VALERIO VIDALI

THE KING'S SHIP

Farshore

Once, a long time ago, there lived a rich and powerful king.
His kingdom stretched through a vast forest all the way to the sea.
His palace was decorated with beautiful marble statues and
many cannons kept it safe and secure.

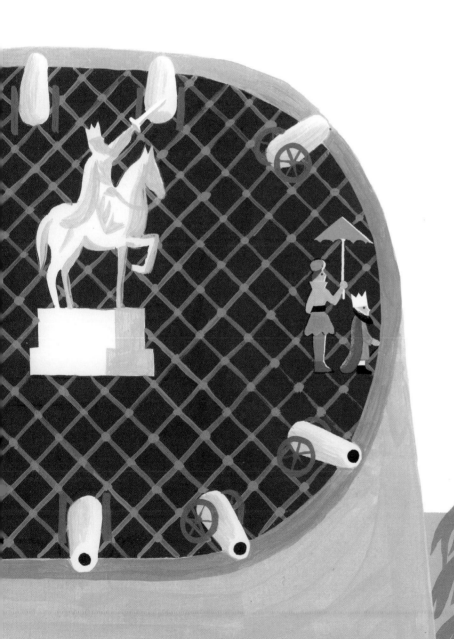

The king had everything he wanted,
apart from . . .

a ship!

The king's advisor summoned
every carpenter in the land:
"Build a **great ship** for the king!"

The carpenters bowed down.

"We will build

a great ship.

We will cut down

the tallest trees."

But the ship they made was not big enough.

The king's advisor summoned
the carpenters again:
"Build a **bigger ship** for the king!"

The carpenters bowed down.

"We will build

a bigger ship.

We will cut down

all the trees."

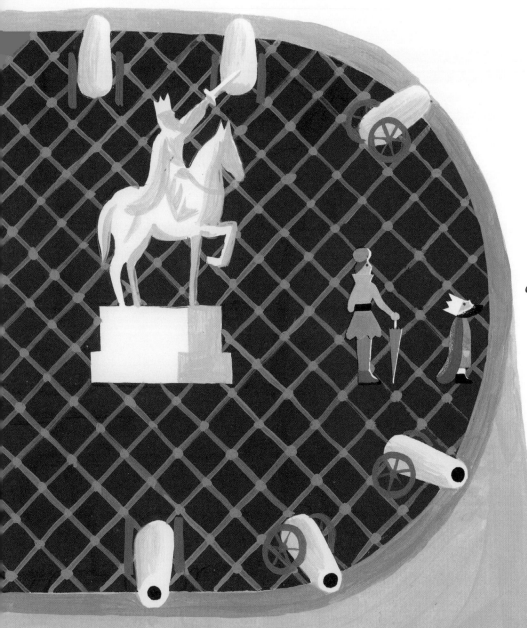

"Hmmm . . ."

Now the king's ship was big.
But it lacked something . . .

The king's advisor summoned
all the soldiers in the land:
"Cannons! We need lots of cannons.
The king's ship isn't **terrifying** enough!"

The soldiers saluted.

"We'll collect

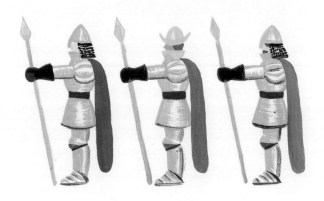

each cannon

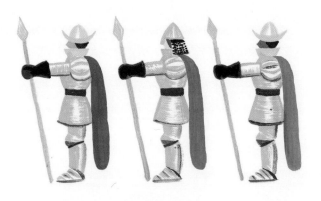

and put it

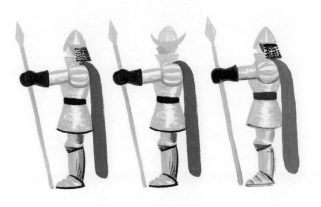

on the ship!"

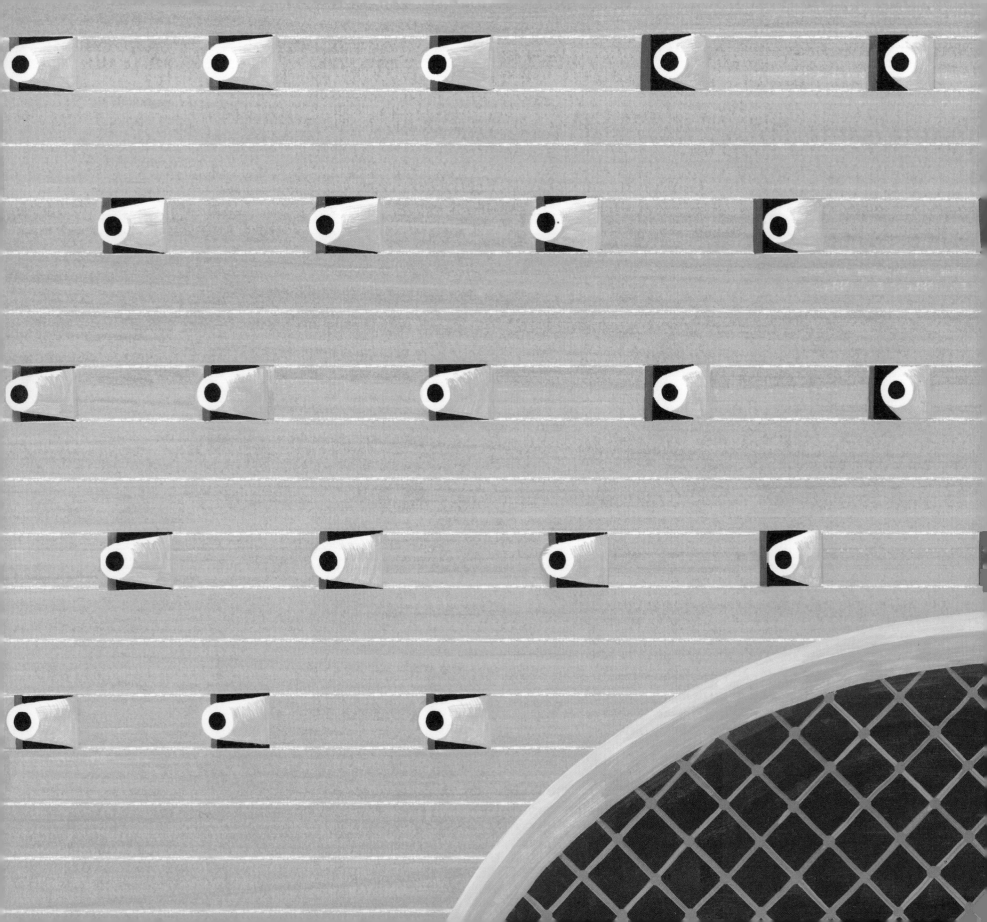

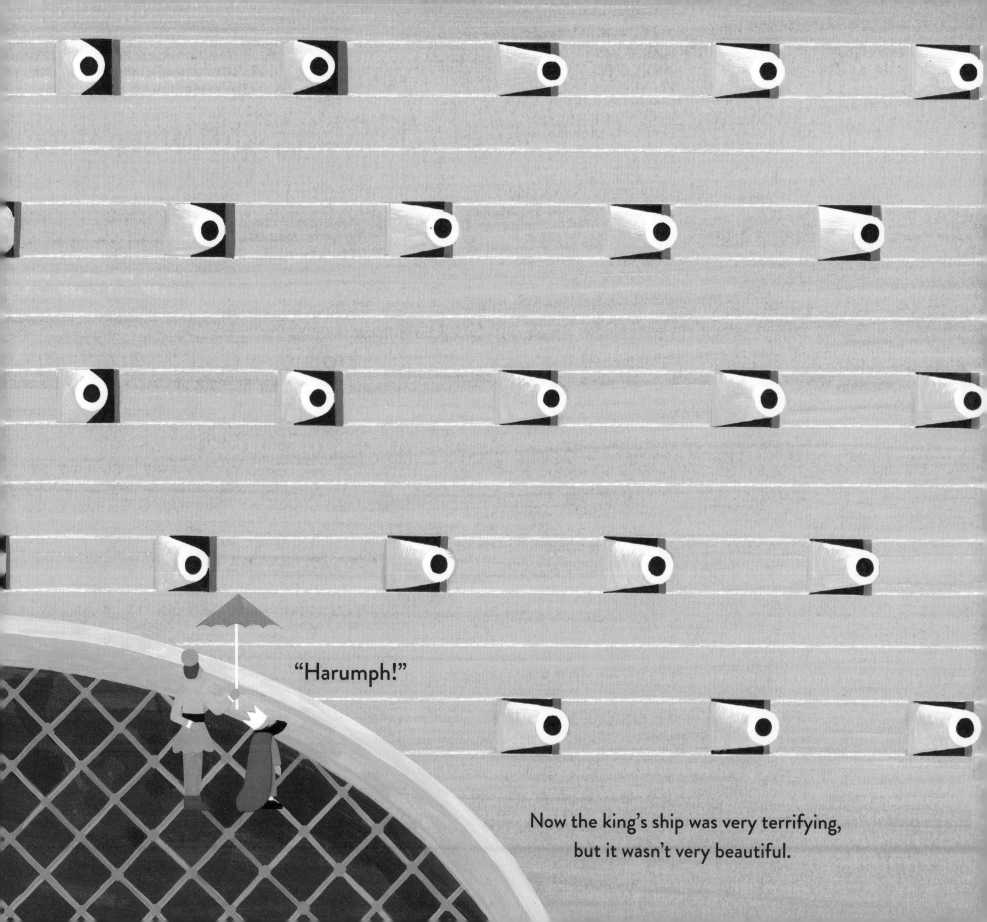

"Harumph!"

Now the king's ship was very terrifying,
but it wasn't very beautiful.

The king's advisor summoned
all the servants in the palace:
"The king's ship isn't **beautiful** enough.
We need marble statues!"

The servants doffed their caps.

"We will

put every

statue on

the ship!"

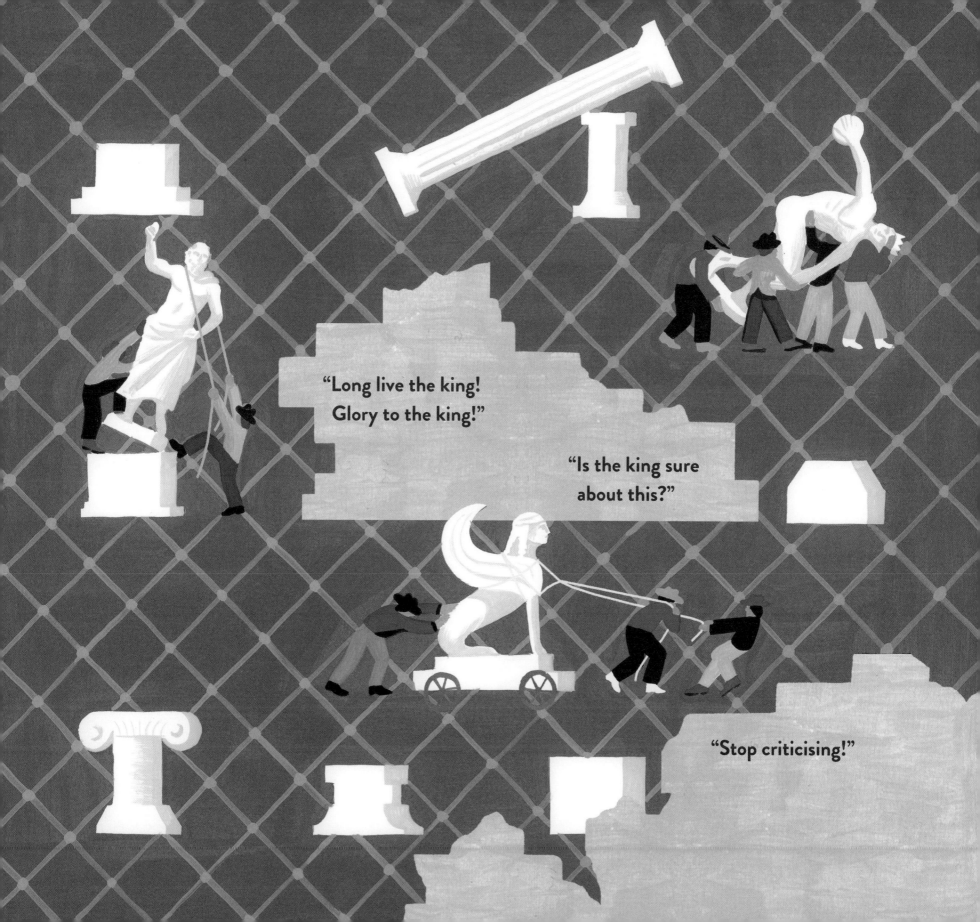

The king's ship was finished at last.
It was big.
It was terrifying
It was beautiful.
The king was very happy.

"Yay!"

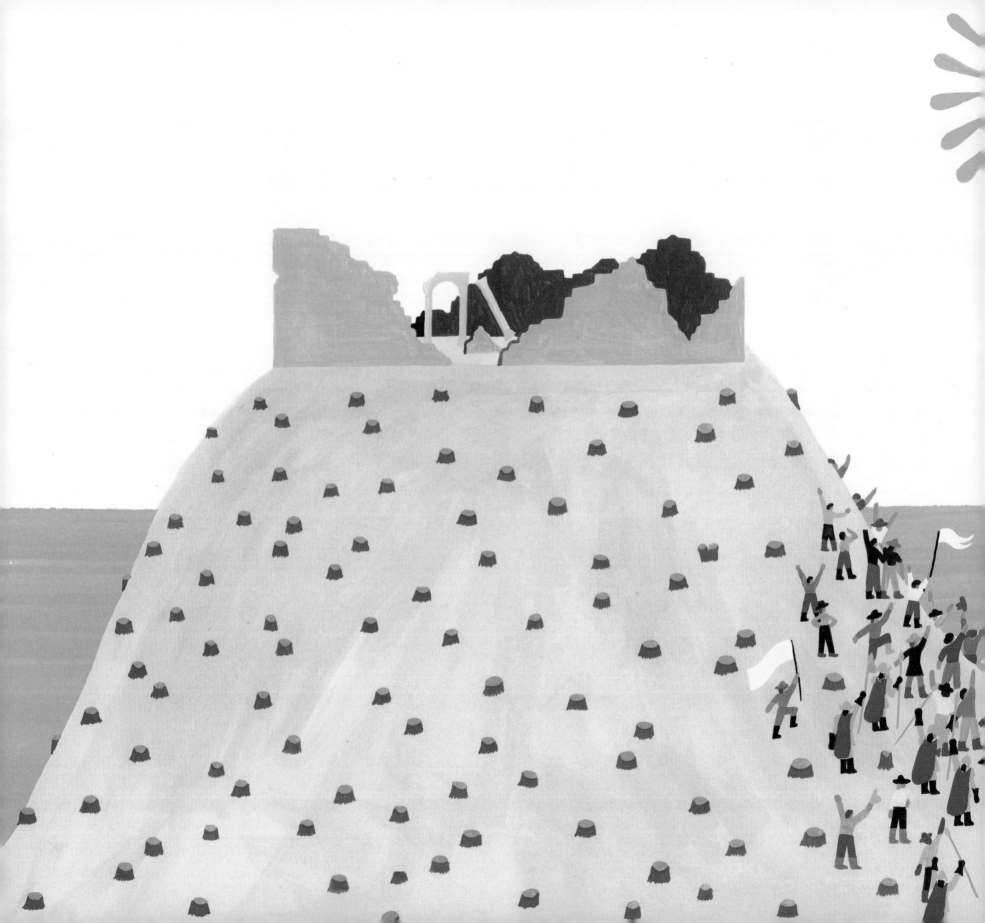

The king's advisor summoned the carpenters,
the soldiers and the servants:
"Admire the king's ship!"

"Admire the firepower of his cannons!
Admire the beauty of his statues!
Admire–"

A light breeze blew and
suddenly the ship began to tilt.

"Uh-oh . . ."

Plop!

The king's big, terrifying, beautiful and very heavy ship had sunk.

NOTE FROM VALERIO VIDALI

The inspiration for this picture book comes from the true history of the *Vasa*, a 17th-century Swedish warship. At the time of its construction, Sweden was at war with Poland, and the *Vasa* was intended as a symbol of the king's greatness and ambition. Upon completion, the *Vasa* was the biggest and most powerfully armed vessel in the world. It was covered with colourful sculptures, paintings and other treasures, and it was magnificent.

However, the *Vasa* was dangerously unstable and it sank on its maiden voyage less than a mile outside Stockholm's harbour. Stockholm is the capital of Sweden.